NOT NOW, NOOR!

Farhana Islam ✦ Nabila Adani

PUFFIN

My ammu's hijab is **NOT** her hair.

It's **NOT** a towel

and it definitely **ISN'T** a hat.

NOT NOW, NOOR!

To the children who were never afraid to ask – F. I.

For my mama, my Aisha and Ninda, my sister – N. A.

PUFFIN BOOKS

UK | USA | Canada | Ireland | Australia
India | New Zealand | South Africa

Puffin Books is part of the Penguin Random House group of companies
whose addresses can be found at global.penguinrandomhouse.com.

www.penguin.co.uk   www.puffin.co.uk   www.ladybird.co.uk

 Penguin
Random House
UK

First published 2023
001

Text copyright © Farhana Islam, 2023
Illustrations copyright © Nabila Adani, 2023

The moral right of the author and illustrator has been asserted

Printed in China

The authorized representative in the EEA is Penguin Random House Ireland,
Morrison Chambers, 32 Nassau Street, Dublin D02 YH68

A CIP catalogue record for this book is available from the British Library

ISBN: 978-0-241-55247-6

All correspondence to: Puffin Books, Penguin Random House Children's,
One Embassy Gardens, 8 Viaduct Gardens, London SW11 7BW

MIX
Paper from
responsible sources
FSC® C018179
FSC
www.fsc.org

She wears it
like this . . .

She wears it
like that . . .

Sometimes
like this.

And sometimes like that.

But NEVER
like this

and NEVER
like that.

Ammu's hijab looks nothing like my nanu's hijab
and not at all like my dadu's hijab.

It's almost like my auntie Salma's hijab
and smells EXACTLY like my sister's hijab.

Ammu's hijab is beautiful.
Just like my ammu.

But why do Ammu (and Affa and Auntie Salma and Dadu and
Nanu) wear a hijab? The more I thought, the more I wondered . . .
My head was always full of questions.

So I decided to ask the coolest hijabi I know. My affa.
She loved to hear ALL of my questions, even when
it was my MILLIONTH one of the day.

"Is it because you like to hide your snacks?"
(And then save the crumbs for later?)

"Or is it so nobody sees your enormous ears?"
(They really are GIGANTIC.)

But Affa was too busy being cool.
"Not now, Noor . . . Go ask somebody else!"

Perhaps Auntie Salma would tell me – after all, she is the toughest hijabi I know. AND the fiercest one too. She's the STRICTEST teacher on the whole, entire planet. She knows absolutely EVERYTHING there is to ever know.

"Is it so you
don't catch nits
at school?"

"Or is it because it hides the eyes on the back of your head?"
(Auntie Salma ALWAYS knows
what EVERYBODY is up to.)

But Auntie Salma was too busy being tough.
"Not now, Noor . . . Go ask somebody else!"

So off I marched to find Nanu.
She must be able to tell me!

Nanu is the most curious hijabi I know.
The most secretive and SASSIEST nanu
on the whole, entire planet.

"Is it because you're a super spy and you
have to stay UNDER COVER all the time?

Or maybe it's because you're a TOP secret agent,
always trying to save the world."

But Nanu was too busy being curious.
"Ssssshhhh! Not now, Noor . . .
Go ask somebody else!"

HMMPH.
Not again.
Why would no one
answer me?

So off I stormed to find Dadu.
She had to tell me . . .

Dadu is the quirkiest hijabi I know.
And the SLEEPIEST one too.
But she is the oldest and wisest and kindest.

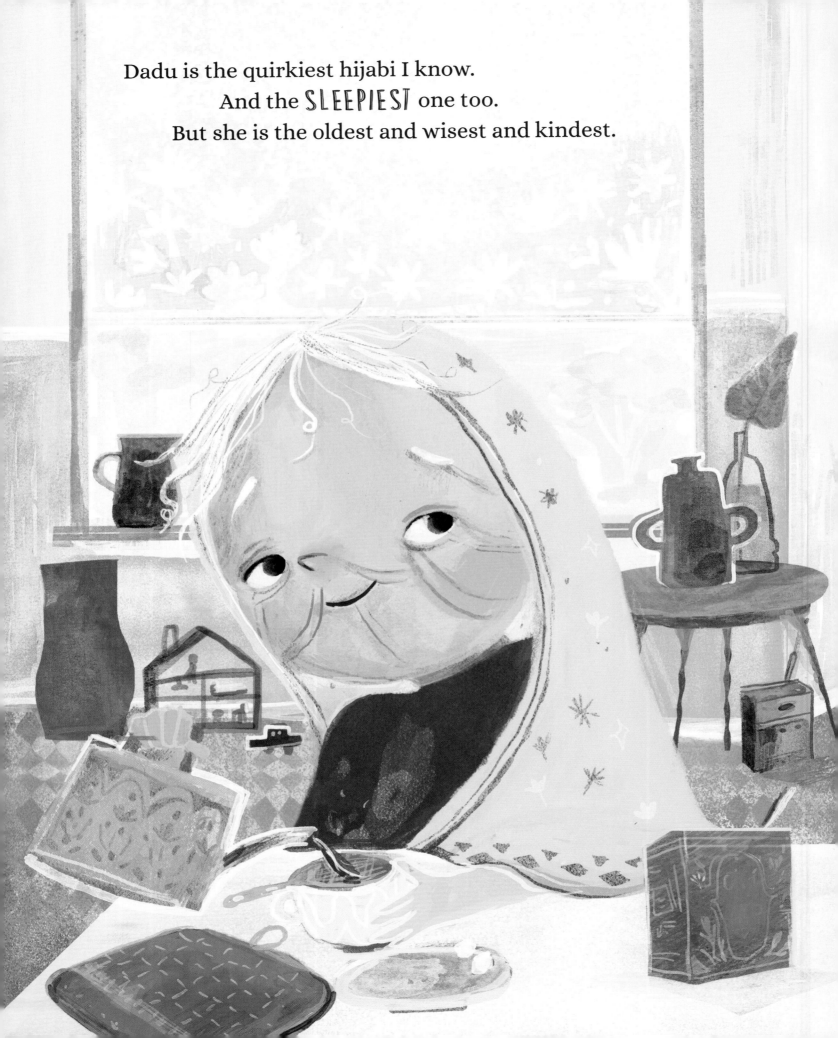

"Is it so you don't have to listen to Dada talk?
Or is it so nobody can see when you're having a bad hair day?"

(Which is EVERY DAY.)

Then Dadu did something
that NOBODY had done.

"Come closer, my Noor.
     I'll tell you all that I know."

I jumped

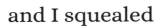

and I squealed

and I scrambled
towards her.

FINALLY.

"Back in my day," she began,
"we used to bathe
with it o–"

All of a sudden, there was a noise.

With a snort and a snuffle, Dadu was out like a light!

My head was all muddled and jumbled and knotty.
It was clear that my dadu had lost the plot.

"Not now, Dadu!" I begged and I pleaded.

WHAT was I to do?

WHO was I to ask?

If hijab was so important,
WHY did no one answer back?

But at that moment something suddenly felt right.
There was only ONE person who would know what to say.
So I hurried off to find the CLEVEREST hijabi I know.

My ammu!

Ammu would have lots of answers
because ammus always do.

"Come now, my Noor . . . I'm so glad you asked!"
Like all ammus, she knew what to say;
she knew what to do.

"We are Muslim women, my Noor. Unapologetic and true.
We are believers. We are dreamers.
We are thinkers. We are leaders.
We can wear our hijabs on our heads like our hearts on our sleeves.
Whether you choose to or not, my Noor,
we are so many things . . .
and we are more than enough.

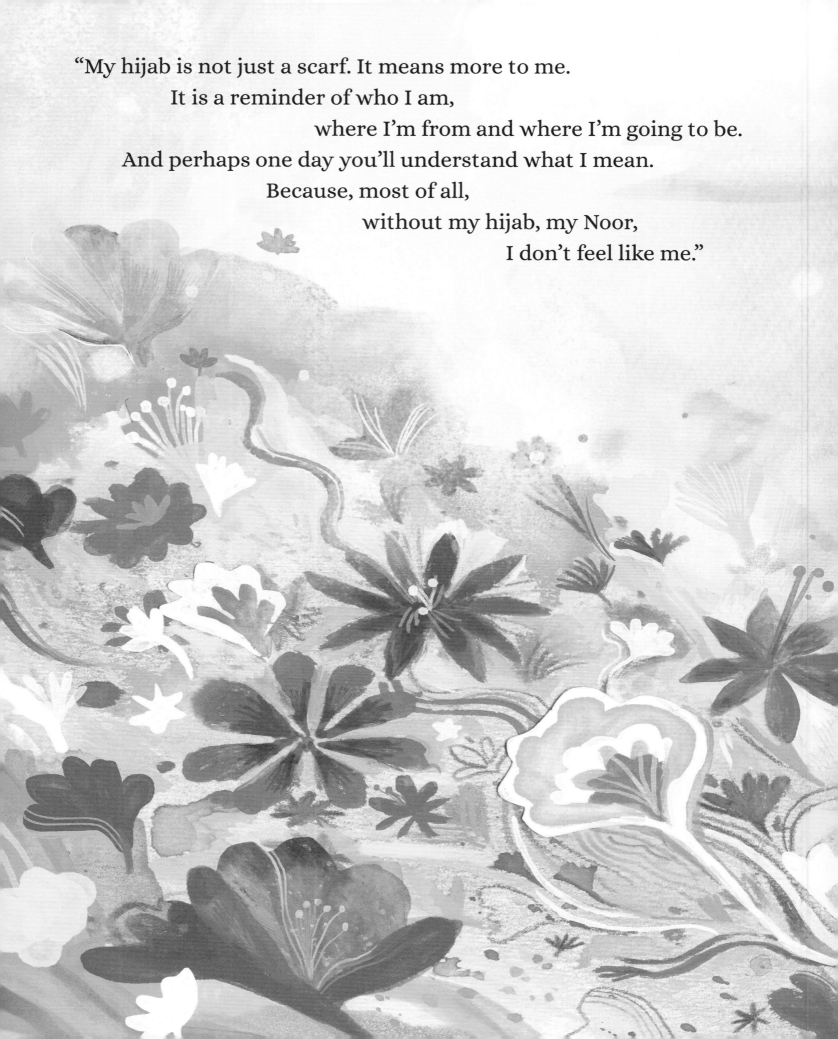

"My hijab is not just a scarf. It means more to me.
It is a reminder of who I am,
where I'm from and where I'm going to be.
And perhaps one day you'll understand what I mean.
Because, most of all,
without my hijab, my Noor,
I don't feel like me."

And there was my answer.

Like all ammus do,
my ammu just knew . . .

And maybe, just maybe, one day
I'll wear a hijab too.